Buffy
the Vampire Slayer

ANGEL

PAST
LIVES

Art by CHRISTIAN ZANIER and ANDREW PEPOY
Colors by DAVE STEWART

ANGEL

based on the television series created by

JOSS WHEDON & DAVID GREENWALT

writers CHRISTOPHER GOLDEN & TOM SNIEGOSKI

pencillers CHRISTIAN ZANIER & CLIFF RICHARDS

inkers JOE PIMENTEL & DIGITAL JUMP

colorist LEE LOUGHRIDGE letterer CLEM ROBINS cover art KEITH WOOD

TITAN
BOOKS

publisher
MIKE RICHARDSON

editor
SCOTT ALLIE
with MICHAEL CARRIGLITTO

collection designer
KEITH WOOD

art director
MARK COX

Alexa Landry and various demons designed by
CHRISTIAN ZANIER

special thanks to
DEBBIE OLSHAN AT FOX LICENSING,
CAROLINE KALLAS AND GEORGE SNYDER AT BUFFY THE VAMPIRE SLAYER

PUBLISHED BY
TITAN BOOKS
144 SOUTHWARK STREET
LONDON SE1 OUP

FIRST EDITION
OCTOBER 2001

A CIP catalogue record for this title is
available from the British Library

ISBN: 1-84023-366-4

Introduction

It had to be big.

On television, when *Buffy the Vampire Slayer* and *Angel* cross over, the producers have to coordinate not one but two armies of people, as well as storylines, and actors' schedules.

We didn't have to do that.

From the very start, we needed to take advantage of the fact that while, as a general rule, the show might have Buffy come to L.A., or Angel go to Sunnydale, or maybe Oz appear in *Angel* . . . we could do a lot more. We could bring the entire Scooby Gang to Los Angeles, to mix with Angel and Cordelia and Wesley for the first time since those characters had been spun off from the original series into its spawn.

So . . . we had that going for us. But, honestly, it wasn't going to be enough. As I said, if we were going to bother doing this thing at all, it had to be bigger than that. Certainly anytime you put Buffy and Angel in a room together, their past resonates in their every interaction. Bringing Giles in helps also, because, let's not forget, once upon a time Angel murdered his girlfriend and mercilessly tortured him. In truth, you could pick almost any combination of characters from these two series, put them together, and come up with a fascinating dynamic.

But all of that is sub-plot, theme, character. Wonderful stuff, but what about the plot?

The only thing Tom Sniegoski and I knew as we set out was that we wanted the story to take place in L.A. rather than Sunnydale, because, let's face it, that was more fun. More than likely, Angel wasn't going to call Buffy for help even if he was staked out like Gulliver on the beach and the sun was rising. Which meant that Angel had to be in some serious trouble, and Cordelia and Wesley had to be so outmatched that their only choice was to call Buffy.

Hmmm. Someone's gotta open up a serious can of whupass on Angel. That could be fun.

Still, though, not much of a story. So why don't I let you in on a little secret. Tom and I love Giles. His character is rich with potential, and yet so horribly underused, that we wanted to include him. Once we started to talk about that, ideas began to flow. Questions began to arise.

What's The Council of Watchers been up to since Buffy sent them packing? How have they dealt with what must be quite an embarrassment in the international supernatural espionage community?

What if the hunter who is after Angel also has ties to Giles?

What if the hunter who is after Angel is hunting him for a damn good reason, one no one could possibly argue with?

Angel did a lot of horrible things in the more than a century before he was cursed with the return of his soul. It only stands to reason that there might still be people, beings, entities out there who bear him a serious grudge for those actions.

Well . . . there isn't a whole lot more I can say about that without giving everything away. As an interesting note, though, I should point out that I've written before about how writers should never throw good ideas away because chances are you'll get a chance to use them eventually.

Tom and I had pitched an idea for an issue of the monthly *Angel* comic book called "The Fearless Vampire Killer," the title an homage to a classic B-movie. The story took place in the 1800s when Angel was the scourge of Europe. It was meant to be a stand-alone story illustrating just how unrepentantly evil our hero had been once upon a time. Unfortunately, the Powers That Be decided that they didn't want us to ever do a story in which Angel was shown only as his evil self. It was one thing, apparently, to acknowledge his past, but no one wanted to dwell on it.

We were pretty disappointed, I have to confess.

Then "Past Lives" came up. During our conversations, Tom and I realized that the story meant for "The Fearless Vampire Killer" was the final piece of the puzzle that would make this crossover event the kind of story we knew it could be. In our minds, it was the sort of thing that they would never be able to do on television, but that might happen if they ever decide to make that *Buffy* movie that has been rumored for so long.

Not *this* story, of course. But a story that includes all of your favorite characters and has a special-effects budget that would allow the producers to do whatever they wanted to do.

On that front, to give credit where credit is due, the demons in "Past Lives" are a little more inventive than you might have found in previous stories we've done for this mythos. That was Tom. He wanted to make sure they were different. I think he – and the art team – succeeded, but you'll have to be the judge of that.

Finally, since we're giving out credit, this story would not be nearly as effective were it not for the amazing efforts of the entire art team, particularly pencilers Cliff Richards and Christian Zanier, both of whom turned in some of their best work for "Past Lives." The character of Alexa Landry was staked out as the perfect territory for Christian to showcase his talents as a "Bad Girl" artist, which he had little opportunity to do in the regular *Angel* series. You'll see within what a stellar job he did with her design. When circumstances prevented Christian from drawing the entire crossover, Cliff Richards jumped in and did some absolutely wonderful work.

By now, you've probably guessed that Sniegoski and I had a lot of fun on this project.

We hope you do, too.

– Christopher Golden

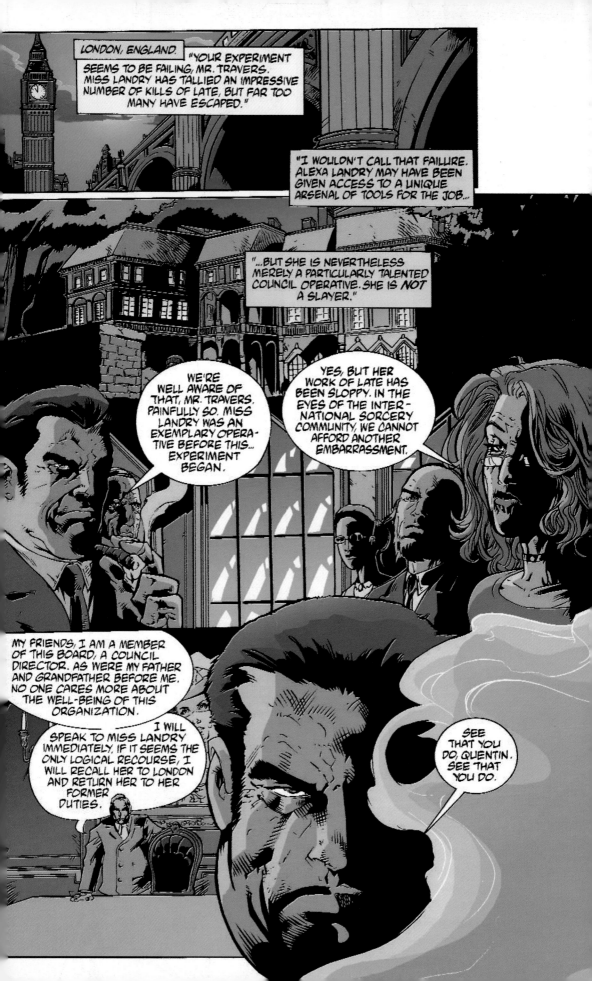

GONNA HAVE TO FIX THAT DOOR AGAIN.

CORDELIA! WESLEY!

YOU'RE PROBABLY GOING TO WANT TO LAY LOW FOR A WHILE.

GO HOME. I'LL CALL YOU WHEN THIS IS ALL OVER.

WHEN IT'S...

NO, SERIOUSLY, BUFF. HELP ME OUT.

WE KNOW HELLMOUTH IS TO DEMONS WHAT A DONUT SHOP IS TO COPS, RIGHT? BUT *HELLO?* SLAYER IN TOWN YOU'VE BEEN HERE LONG ENOUGH FOR THEM TO HAVE FIGURED IT OUT.

THAT SEXY HELLMOUTH GLOW? PRETTY MUCH THE DEADLY LURE OF THE BACKYARD BUG ZAPPER AS LONG AS YOU'RE AROUND. SO WHY DO THEY KEEP COMING?

WHAT CAN I SAY, XAND? MONSTERS. JUST NOT THAT BRIGHT.

ACTUALLY, SOME OF THEM ARE EXTREMELY INTELLIGENT. JUST, Y'KNOW, TOO FULL OF THEIR OWN DEMON-Y SELVES TO BE AFRAID.

FOR SOME, IT COULD BE THAT THE PULL OF THE HELLMOUTH IS SIMPLY STRONGER THAN THEIR FEAR. OTHERS... I JUST DON'T UNDERSTAND.

TELL ME ABOUT IT. I TOLD YOU GUYS ABOUT THE BONE-HEAD WITH THE SWORD THE OTHER DAY.

ON THE RUN FROM SOME DEMON HUNTER, SO HE COMES HERE? WE CAN SAFELY ASSUME *NOT* ON THE HONOR ROLL AT THE GHOUL SCHOOL.

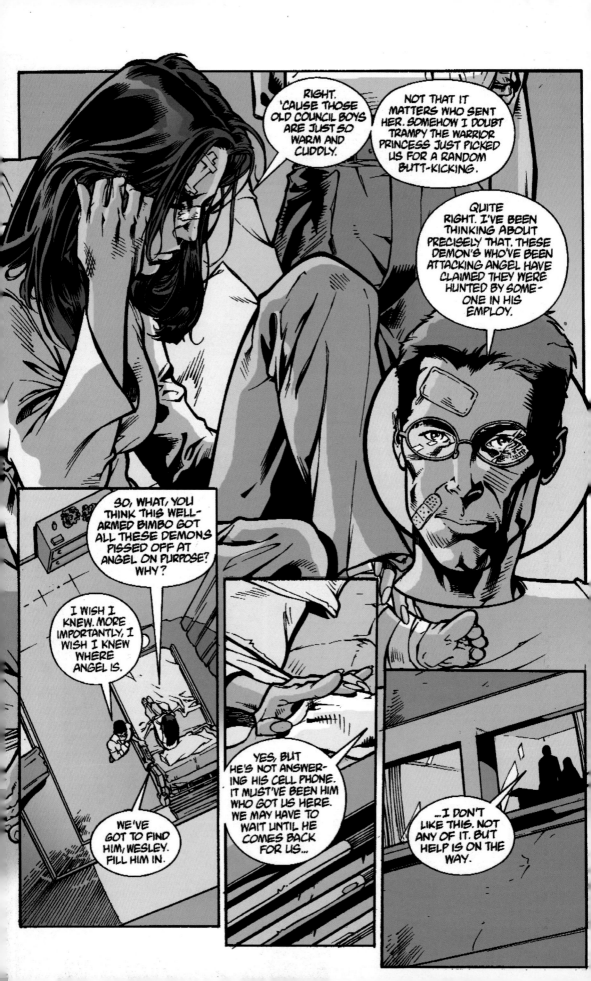

NOT THAT I WAS EAVESDROPPING, BUT HELLO? YOU AND THIS DEMON HUNTER CHICK USED TO HAVE A THING?

DON'T YOU EVER KNOCK?

WANT ME TO PRETEND I DIDN'T HEAR THAT?

FOR A BRIEF PERIOD, WHEN SHE FIRST BECAME AN OPERATIVE FOR THE COUNCIL, I WAS INDEED...INVOLVED WITH ALEXA LANDRY.

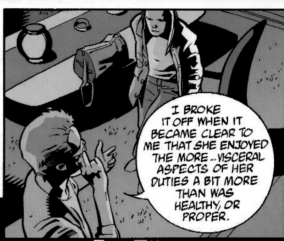

I BROKE IT OFF WHEN IT BECAME CLEAR TO ME THAT SHE ENJOYED THE MORE...VISCERAL ASPECTS OF HER DUTIES A BIT MORE THAN WAS HEALTHY, OR PROPER.

THE PAST ALWAYS COMES BACK TO HAUNT US.

INDEED.

TARA AND I HAVE SOME WITCHY *MISSION: IMPOSSIBLE* OR OTHER, 'CAUSE, YOU KNOW, OF THE MAGIC.

AND, XAND, SHE WANTS YOU AND ANYA TO LOOK OUT FOR WESLEY AND CORDELIA. IT'S PRETTY OBVIOUS THAT THIS WOMAN HAS MADE THEM TARGETS TOO.

AND... RILEY? I DIDN'T HEAR RILEY IN THERE.

RIGHT. WHICH WOULD BE BECAUSE BUFFY NEEDS SOMEONE TO HOLD DOWN THE FORT HERE, AND YOU'RE THE ONLY ONE SHE TRUSTS TO DO THAT. HOLD IT. THE FORT, I MEAN.

THAT'S RIDICU-LOUS. I COULD HOLD THE FORT. WE'VE HELD THE FORT BEFORE. I'M GOOD WITH THE FORT.

XANDER, DON'T BE OBTUSE. BUFFY DOESN'T WANT RILEY TO COME TO LOS ANGELES BECAUSE SHE USED TO HAVE SEX WITH ANGEL, AND SHE HAS SEX WITH RILEY NOW.

GREAT. THANKS FOR CLEARING THAT UP, ANYA. REALLY.

THE LANDRY ESTATE, SHEFFIELD, GREAT BRITAIN.

1854.

THE FIRST TIME ANDREW LANDRY SAW A VAMPIRE HE WAS FOURTEEN YEARS OLD. HE HAS BEEN HUNTING THEM EVER SINCE.

THIRTEEN YEARS AGO, HIS QUEST WAS FOREVER ALTERED.

ANDREW LANDRY HAD THOUGHT HIM-SELF A HERO, THEN.

BUT A HERO WOULD HAVE SAVED THEM.

MARGARET? WHY IS IT DARK? IS THE LITTLE ONE ALREADY ASLEEP?

LOVELY PLACE YOU'VE GOT HERE, SIR ANDREW. AN ADORABLE FAMILY...

...AND THE MOST GULLIBLE SERVANTS.

YOUNG ELIZABETH THOUGHT I LOVED HER. CAN YOU IMAGINE?

HSSSS

MARGARET, NO!

YOUR MUM AND DA ARE HAVING A WEE SPAT, LITTLE ALEX. NOTHING TO BE TROUBLED ABOUT.

ANGELUS! BY ALL THAT IS SACRED--

HEY. VISITING HOURS OVER YET, OR CAN I COME IN?

ANGEL! THANK THE LORD. WHEN WE HADN'T HEARD FROM YOU, WE THOUGHT THE WORST.

OR, AT LEAST, WE THOUGHT SIGOURNEY WEAVER HAD CAUGHT UP WITH YOU.

WHICH, GIVEN HOW CRAPPY YOU LOOK, WAS APPARENTLY NOT TOO FAR FROM THE TRUTH.

THANKS FOR THE VOTE OF CONFIDENCE, CORDELIA. AND I'M FINE, BY THE WAY. RELIEVED TO SEE THAT YOU TWO ARE IN ONE PIECE. MORE OR LESS.

NOW WE'VE JUST GOT TO FIGURE OUT WHO WE'RE DEALING WITH HERE.

ACTUALLY, ANGEL, WE ALREADY KNOW. SHE'S A COUNCIL OPERATIVE, THOUGH I'VE NO IDEA WHY SHE SEEMS TO HAVE FOCUSED HER ENERGIES ON YOU. HER NAME IS ALEXA LANDRY.

SHE'S A LANDRY?

NO WONDER SHE WANTS TO KILL ME.

YOU DON'T HAVE TO DO THIS, ALEXA. ANGEL HAS A HUMAN SOUL, AND HE SUFFERS FOR THE SINS OF THE DEMON WITHIN HIM. THE PAST IS A TEACHER, BUT FOR YOU IT HAS BEEN A PRISON.

IT'S ALL RIGHT, GILES. THIS IS ALL ON ME. I'LL TAKE IT FROM HERE.

MY WHOLE LIFE HAS LED UP TO THIS MOMENT, ANGELUS. NOW YOU DIE!

ONLY IF I "PULL MY PUNCHES."

AND I WON'T.

KRAAK!

YOU BROKE IT. YOU...HURT ME.

AAA'EE!

YOU'RE GOING DOWN A DARK ROAD, ALEXA. WHATEVER YOUR REASONS, YOU'VE GONE TOO FAR NOW. BUT IT ISN'T TOO LATE TO TURN BACK. NOT YET. YOU CAN STILL--

IT WAS TOO LATE THE DAY I WAS BORN.

THE END